THE JOSHUA CITADEL,

THE LAST BATTLE

GIACOMO GIAMMATTEO

INFERNO PUBLISHING COMPANY

Print ISBN 978-1-940313-61-0

Electronic ISBN 978-1-940313-49-8

❀ Created with Vellum

INTRODUCTION

Time —the not too distant future —Post Apocalypse

Place—a world not unlike our own

The tale I tell is one of woe: a war that has lasted for centuries; a war where the casualties numbered in the billions, if not more; most importantly, a war that could have been avoided.

God knows we tried. How many peace initiatives went unanswered? How many times did we stay our hand, refusing to attack or seek vengeance for unjust acts?

But they wouldn't let us live in peace. They wouldn't let us sit idly by. A vicious race they were. Warriors to the core. A bloodthirsty, greedy race.

"How did it start, Grandfather?"

Ox might have shed tears if he had any. But the wars had taken so much of him: a wife, two daughters, all his friends. "They were a relentless enemy, child. An unremitting and unforgiving foe."

PROLOGUE

Time—Pre Apocalypse

Cacid raced down the corridor, anxious about facing Commander Ribo. Ribo's lack of tolerance for failure was legendary. Cacid rounded the bend and almost ran into her. Startled, Cacid adjusted her posture and saluted.

"They're gone, sir!" It took all she had to restrain herself, maintain the military decorum. "I mean goddamn...they're all fu..." A brief pause to recompose. "Sorry, sir. Won't happen again."

"Ease it along, soldier. Who's gone? Tell it from the beginning."

Cacid felt on fire, like the time they had infiltrated the Joshua citadel and the enemy unleashed the heat on them. She almost didn't make it that day—wouldn't have if not for Commander Ribo, the officer she addressed.

"Sir, we had just finished scouting one of their newest fortresses— actually on our way back—when Pro discovered a breach in one of the other citadels. I believe it was the Robbins citadel, sir." Glee raced through her, quickly chased by guilt.

"I know we shouldn't have done it, sir, but we all agreed we couldn't pass it up. So we went in. All of us. Three full patrols. We got through all right, no sign of security. No hint that we were spotted. But about halfway through, they came." Cacid felt dry, parched. "Sir, I think I need some fluids. If you don't mind—"

"You'll live without fluids. Your patrol obviously did not fare so well. Continue. I need to know what happened."

Ribo's words stung. If Cacid had thought to find comfort in Commander Ribo, she had sorely misjudged. "Sorry, sir. Anyway, they hit us near the cavern, the big one. And they came from all angles. We thought we had gotten in clean, but obviously not. An ambush, sir. B's, some of their Elite units, even the Quads. They were waiting like vipers, sir. Surrounded us. They had even positioned themselves above us. We didn't have a chance. I got about three of the B's, then jumped in the river and headed upstream. I know two of the guys followed me—Pro, for one, and maybe Edge, but I lost them after a while. They never were the fastest swimmers, sir."

"How did you get out?"

"Launched, sir. I used an irritant and launched."

Commander Ribo let silence fill the air. One of her famous pauses, or infamous, if you happened to be on the receiving end.

Cacid fidgeted, but only in her mind; she didn't dare move. She knew it had only been a moment or two, but it seemed like forever. Finally, Ribo broke the torture.

"All dead, then? All but you?"

Goddamn, bastard. What a way to put it, but then, Ribo always did have a way of making you feel like shit. "Yes, sir. As far as I know, they're all dead. There is a chance that Pro and Edge made it out, but I don't know." Cacid figured she might as well drive the last nail in herself. "So, unless they made it, everyone is dead, but me."

~

"Dismissed," Ribo said, no emotion in her voice.

As Cacid left, Ribo pondered her report. Yet another example of advanced technology, or, meticulous security. *Or treachery,* she thought, and wondered anew how Cacid had made it through two massacres as the lone survivor, or one of the only survivors.

I'll need to call a meeting. Need research in on this.

THINK TANKS

Commander Ribo moved through the compound at her usual pace, neither slow nor hurried. The commander wore standard military garb flung over a pale body, and what some called a misshapen head, though others claimed her ego caused the deformities.

Ribo heard it all; nothing on this compound went unnoticed or unreported. She kept her reputation intact by arriving to any meeting at the last minute. Late was never an option for her but then, neither was early. If a meeting was at 10:52, she would *not* arrive at 10:51.

Ribo scanned the group: Nuc was there. Cacid and De, too. And all the key researchers, including the highly respected Doctor Phage, along with his think-tank boys. People still referred to them as the think-tank boys, even though two-thirds of them were now of the opposite gender.

"Good morning, Commander Ribo. We were just about to—"

"I'll control this meeting, Phage. You might be hot shit in this lab, but I'm running an army, and I need some goddamned answers."

Phage folded his hands and let them slide down beneath what would have been a stomach—if he had one. And if there had been any color in him, it disappeared with Commander Ribo's reprimand. "Of course, Commander." His apology barely reached across the room.

"I'm sure Cacid has filled you in on her latest failure, so—"

Ribo thought she heard a snicker from one of the researchers. A twisting top could not have spun around faster than her head. "Funny, mister?" Her questions could skewer a person.

"No, sir," the cowering lab tech replied.

"No, I guess it's not. Fact is, you won't think it's funny at all, because you're going in, mister."

The tech nearly choked. "Pardon, sir? But I'm—"

"You'll be *goddamned* what I tell you to be. If I tell you to be a mound of shit, mister, I expect you to curl up and stink." Ribo waited until the tech nodded. "Report to duty with Captain Teins at once."

The tech started to leave, looking back at Doctor Phage in a pleading manner.

"Leave that lab coat, mister. Blood doesn't mix well with white." As the portal slid open, then shut, Ribo turned back to face the group.

That should get their attention.

"I was talking about Cacid before the disturbance. And it isn't a reflection on her that I used the word *failure*. Fail, she did, but so has every other mission we've undertaken. It's nothing for her to be ashamed of, and nothing for any of you to chortle about. It's information. That's all. Now, let's see what we can do with that information." Ribo looked across the room.

An unnamed lab tech rose from his seat like a first-grader. Ribo half expected him to raise his hand and begin waving it. "We all know their security is impenetrable, Commander Ribo. Before we do anything we have to find a way in."

Ribo saw Nuc itching to respond. "Nuc, your opinion?"

Nuc, a veteran of six campaigns, had an unorthodox shape. Some called him a corkscrew, others a spring, but everyone agreed that the way he could twist his body, made him resemble something other than normal. He was darker than most, too. Darker than all her officers except Ox.

Ribo had a mix of colors in her command, ranging from lily white to dark to dark-as-night, as Ox liked to say. But Ox was darker than night. And when he lined up next to De he made black look bright.

"The citadels are not impenetrable. We can get in." Nuc scanned the group to see if anyone would contest his statement. He wasn't comfortable with the lab people; his education had been in the field. "Getting in is not the problem, it's getting in undetected. Detection is the key. They know we're in there almost as soon as we enter. If we could have even a few hours, we'd be set."

He heard some rumblings in the group and thought he knew what they were saying. "I'm not afraid to die, Commander. You know that. But if we don't find something..."

He let the words sink in. He felt certain that everyone knew what he was talking about. No one, but no one wanted to face Thunder Quads or Battle Cells. And if the alarm was raised, that's exactly what they would face—that and a host of other assaults.

Questions poured forth from all sides. Ribo let them talk, chew things over. It was good to have the soldiers mix with the lab and think-tank guys. Made for creative thoughts.

As she was about ready to continue, Little Pro walked in, and he looked as if he'd been through more than a wringer.

Ribo turned and displayed surprise. "Pro! Where have you been? We thought you were dead."

"Sorry about that. I was delayed getting home. Had to keep evading them. I haven't even reported in to Cacid yet."

Ribo hugged him. "No worries. I'll keep her informed. We're just glad to have you back. Now, take a seat and fill me in while the rest of these soldiers and techies chat."

R ibo kept herself busy for almost an hour, then decided it was time to stir things up and give them something to chew on. "All right. Listen up!"

When she had everyone's attention, she continued. "What's been the problem?"

Nuc was the first one to speak up. "Like I said earlier, it's detection. Every time we go in, they're ready. Somehow they identify us. Their tracers pick us up, then we're dead."

Doctor Phage chimed in with a thought. "We *must* know how the defense is structured. If we can find out how they do it, then we can devise a plan to get around it."

"Let's send out a research mission," Nuc said. "Maybe we can gather the data we need to make the strike."

"I'll put someone on it," Commander Ribo said.

"I'll go," Nuc said.

"No. I've got just the person for this. She might even scare a Quad or two into surrendering."

Nuc would have twisted into a smile, but Ribs might have his ass for it. Instead, he smiled.

Must be Teins.

CAPTAIN TEINS

Captain Teins stood at the front of the room, addressing a group of recruits. They were green as hell, not ready for battle. She paced back and forth, arms folded behind her.

"My name is Captain Teins—that's pronounced tines—like mines or fines. The first son of a whore that calls me Captain Teens is gonna get a thirteen-year-old shoved up their ass. Got that?"

Teins could be brutal when irked, so everyone avoided riling her. "Yes, sir, Captain Teins." The united response echoed like the clang of metal in an empty warehouse.

"You have all been selected for one specific reason—your ability to survive hostile conditions, at least *simulated* hostile conditions. Our mission will take us into the most hostile territory there is—Citadel Central." She heard the murmurings, and cast a frozen glare over the group, silencing them.

"We will probably all die. I know most of us will. But that's okay. All we need to do is get in, get the information the think-tank boys need, and make sure at least one of us gets out to deliver it." Teins paced the front line, waiting for questions that never came.

Tough, these kids are. But they don't know what tough is yet. No worry, they'll soon learn.

"All right, go kiss you spouses, kids, parents, pets, or whatever else means anything to you, because it's probable that you won't be back. Tomorrow at 06:00 we meet here." Teins turned to face them, then saluted. "Dismissed!"

Teins watched them leave. Brave kids, one and all. And she had to be the one to send them off to die. How many had she sent to their death? Too many, that's for sure. Well, it would likely be the last time for that. There would be no more after this mission. Teins shuffled all the way to Ribo's headquarters. She walked in, not bothering to knock. "You wanted to see me, sir?"

Commander Ribo's mind was like a central network computer. Things were always moving around in there, getting analyzed, digested, reworked. "Are you ready, Teins? This is an important mission. And it's one we can't afford to screw up."

"We're ready, sir."

"I know *you* are, Teins. I meant are your troops ready. I watched when you told them. A few...well, I thought I detected fear in a few of them."

Teins sought the calmness that hid in the recesses of her mind. "Sir, the only ones I worry about are the ones who *aren't* afraid. They're the ones who might screw up. I'd rather have them afraid going in than have fear suddenly hit them during the middle of a mission."

Ribo didn't respond.

Teins risked it all then. Showing her hand meant Ribo might take the assignment from her. "Sir..."

"Yes, Captain?"

"Sir, I've recorded a few thoughts. Things that...well, things that might be said if I don't make it back. The way I'd like to be remembered."

"You'll be all right, Teins, I'll take care of it." Ribo looked at her. "And don't worry, you'll be back."

"Yes, sir."

Ribo wanted to change the subject. *Needed* to change the subject. "Have you thought about how you'll go in?"

"Yes, sir. I looked at all the maps. We have a few options, but I think I'll take them in at the core. Thought I'd use a launcher and go in where they least expect us."

"A launcher? Through the air filtration system?"

"Yes, sir." Teins moved forward. "I know what you're going to say, sir. And it is well guarded, but it's also where they won't expect us. They definitely anticipate an attack, especially after all of the raids we've pulled these past few months. So with that knowledge, I think we can assume that all entries will have beefed-up security. I think my best chance is here." Teins indicated the ducts leading to the air filtration systems.

Ribo thought for a moment, then agreed. "All right, Captain. It's your call."

"Thank you, sir," she said, and turned to leave.

"Teins," Ribo called, "come back to us, will you? I need soldiers like you to win this war."

"I'll do my best, sir. You can count on that." Before she left, she turned to Ribo one more time. "Sir, no matter what, one of us will be back to report. That, you can definitely count on."

Teins shined, everything on her clean and polished, brilliant even in false light. Teins sparkled in bioluminescense. She would not go out looking the slob.

"Ready?" Ribo asked.

The trip to central wouldn't take long. A flash of light when compared to the length of this war, yet it could mean so much. She had said her farewells to friends, relatives, and lastly, to her parents, still alive despite the shortened life span since the onset of these wars.

"Be careful!" her mom had said. "Love you."

Her father hugged her and tried to hide his tears. He didn't speak for fear he'd give himself away. She knew him well enough to know that. A few long pats, a tousled hair rub, then... "You go get 'em, Tiger," he managed to say without cracking that invisible dam that held the tears in place.

Teins smiled. "I love you, Dad," she said, then hugged him again and went back to lead the mission.

She walked in to a rousing cheer. "Ready, Captain." They gave her an enthusiastic response when she entered, each one snapping to salute.

Teins composed herself, then said, "Follow my lead. Remember, above all else, someone *must* get back with the data. What that means is once we have the data, we stop for nothing or no one. If your best friend goes down, you leave them. If I go down, you leave me. Is that clear?"

"Crystal, Captain."

"All right. Into launch position, soldiers. We're going to Citadel Central."

About halfway there, Teins turned to Cacid. "Maybe we should split up. I take half to Citadel Central, and you go to Citadel Joshua."

"If you think so," Cacid said. She recalculated her position, mapped a new route, then signaled for her troops to follow her lead.

~

"Entry ahead, Captain," the forward scout reported.

"Entry ahead," repeated Teins. "Audible communication is to stop now! Only body signals."

Cavern entrance

Getting in proved to be easy enough, and it even looked as if they had avoided detection, though Teins didn't count on that. Guards were in there somewhere, Teins knew, and they would only get thicker as they neared the command center.

She surveyed the surroundings—dark, but she was still able to identify things. They were in a big cavernous room, though not as big as some she'd been in. Accidentally, she brushed against a wall that felt like leather. Immediately, she signaled to the others.

Careful! Don't touch anything.

She cursed herself for stupidity. The enemy might have sensors in these walls. Three broad shelves, like plateaus, jutted out from an interior wall, fountains dripping from each of them into fresh pools, all connected like canal system. And there was a major fountain dropping into a large pool of liquid of an unidentifiable kind.

cavern drop

Goddamn aliens and their wasteful ways.

They moved slowly through the room until they came to the drop chute. Teins peeked over the edge. *Shit.* It looked scary, and she couldn't even see all the way down. What she could see appeared to be water, but it didn't smell like it.

Everyone on the team knew the drill, though. They would forsake all normal means of descending, as the aliens would be heavily guarded. That left this chute as the best way down.

Teins went first, hooking onto a greasy tube-like structure and easing herself down. On the count of five, with no disturbance noted, one of the soldiers followed. Each one after that obeyed the same ritual. They had to keep switching, from pipes to cables to tube-like objects, but eventually they made it to the data level of command central with no casualties.

Teins scanned the group, counted only seventeen. She signaled *Where's little Proton?* He had been called little Proton due to his spunk and resilience. Before anyone could answer, the enemy soldiers attacked.

B's popped out from behind a pillar near Teins and fired away. Teins deftly avoided them, moving for cover as she did. "Everyone out!" she ordered. "Audibles on! Comm-links on. Get back to the launch site, now!"

A mass of AB's found three of her men as they tried to climb back up the pipes. They locked on and destroyed them within seconds. "Ron, Neurrie, get your men and follow me. We'll try to go out the back exit."

"Quads!" Neurrie shouted, but it was already too late. A huge detachment of Thunder Quads emerged from hiding and came at them. It didn't take long. They got Neurrie and the seven soldiers she had left, then they got Ron and his. Perhaps they knew, perhaps not, but they saved Teins for last. She fought with grim determination, but to no avail. The Quads ripped her apart as if she were a paper doll. As Teins lay dying, with her last gasp of life, she prayed that Ribo would tell her parents what happened. And she prayed that someone would get out to inform Ribo of their failed mission.

~

Up above, clinging to a slippery pipe, little Proton choked back horror. He had never seen Quads before, and he had never seen AB's. Fortunately, they hadn't called in during the last attack.

Carefully, he made his way back up the chute, taking one tiny movement at a time. *Have to get back to headquarters*, he told himself. *Have to report this to Commander Ribo.*

The sounds of slaughter stirred horrible images in his mind. Now he thought he heard worse. Others had told him of Big Macs, the legendary giants among the aliens who supposedly could swallow a soldier whole, but he had never believed them. Now he didn't know. And he was afraid to find out. Proton increased his pace while being careful to maintain silence.

Got to get out of here.

After what seemed like days, he reached the cavernous room at the top of the chute. Scanning the surroundings brought no information about aliens, but then, neither had they seen them below. He couldn't wait there forever, though, so he moved into the room, exercising extreme caution.

By the time he got to the launch site, his pace was at full throttle. Training came to bear as he remembered how to set an irritant, and how to launch properly so as not to get snared by defensive mechanisms. He set the irritant, raced to the site, then launched. As he made good his escape, he wondered how Cacid was making out.

～

Over in Citadel Joshua, Cacid made her way to the cavern. She was bruised, bleeding, and exhausted. They had been attacked shortly after entry, just like they were previously. It was almost as if someone had told them she was coming. She set her irritant and followed a small stream, taking every opportunity to seek cover. If luck was smiling on her—and, if she was quiet—she *may* get home safely.

She followed the stream until she saw light, then carefully made her way to the exit. As she sneaked outside, she wondered how Teins had fared.

CACID'S REPORT

Ribo stormed into Nuc's chambers. "Any of your's back yet?"

"I'm waiting on Cacid's' report now. I don't even know if she made it; I heard there were a lot of casualties."

"Don't wait, Nuc. Find her and get the report. I need information and I don't have time to wait."

~

Nuc burst into Cacid's chambers. "Report!. And then I'll know what's taken you so long."

"I was injured, sir. I spent the last few hours in sick bay, then I thought I'd shower and rest before going to see you. I didn't think you'd mind. I wasn't planning on taking long."

"You thought wrong. Now deliver that report. What happened? Who made it out? Who didn't? And why? I want details, and I want them now."

Cacid lowered her head, looking embarrassed. "The enemy must have developed a new weapon, sir. Either they have a new weapon or they're getting information another way."

"Details, soldier. I can't run an army on reports like this. I need specifics."

Cacid trembled; anxiety appeared to be running rampant through her. "They knew we were coming, sir. They *had* to. They attacked not five minutes after we entered."

"Any survivors?"

"I don't think any of mine made it out, but I don't know about Teins."

"What do you mean? You didn't stay together? I thought you were attacking the same citadel."

"We planned on it, but then we decided to split up. Teins went to Central and I took Joshua."

"And they were waiting in both places?" Nuc asked.

Cacid nodded. "As far as I know. I saw Little Pro earlier. He came to see if I'd made it and told me."

Nuc gave it thought. "That almost rules out a traitor. No one knew you were splitting up, and if the traitor was with you, they wouldn't have warned the enemy only to be killed." Nuc thought more, pacing. "So what is it? What the hell are we looking at?"

"I don't know what it is, exactly, sir, but it seemed as if they had some kind of barrier also. We tried everything, but we couldn't get through the sections safely. We had to detour through some deep caverns. That's where they hit us. And like I said, they were waiting, as if they knew we'd be coming."

Nuc wore a worried look while he paced. He could analyze a report in minutes, sometimes seconds, and when he was done, he either had answers or lots of questions. Lots! This was different; he had no clue.

"You said couldn't get in *safely*. That tells me you got in."

Cacid acknowledged his assumption, but wondered why he asked. "We got in, sir. But we attacked a different citadel than Teins. On the way to the siege we decided to split up, attack from two locations. Remember, I just told you?"

"Was it two locations on the same citadel, or two different citadels? You have to forgive me, but my mind is a mess; I forgot already."

"Different ones, sir. Teins attacked Central and I led an attack into Joshua."

"And you both got in?"

Cacid nodded. "We got in, sir. And according to Pro, Teins and her group did also. But whatever this new system is, has got security attached to it that's unbelievable. Even though we made it in, we found armies waiting to ambush us. It was almost like they *let* us get in so that they could slaughter us."

Cacid noted the skepticism on Nuc. "I mean *waiting*, sir. They *knew* we were coming. I think it was their plan."

A dejected sense arose from Cacid. "They got all of us except for myself and Little Proton. One hundred fifty seven breached their defenses, and none but us made it back."

An understanding seemed to settle on Nuc. Cacid could almost see the realization coming to him, like watching a siege infiltrate a fortress, but this was knowledge infiltrating a mind.

"I think I know how they're doing it," Nuc said. "And if I'm right about that, then I'll know how to destroy their system; in fact, we could even use it to our advantage."

A comm-link signal came from Ribo ordering Nuc to the lab. He paced in silence for a while. "All right, Cacid. You're dismissed."

Nuc entered the lab in the midst of a discussion, a young scientist was talking with one of Nuc's top lieutenants.

"I know the citadels are secure, but why not go through the gates. Surely we could find a way to sneak in when they bring in food and water and air." This came from the scientist sitting near the front.

"We've tried," the lieutenant said. "They monitor gates too closely. Not that we couldn't sneak in, but the alarm system is so tight that they would nail us before we got anywhere. And as of yet, we haven't found any way to disguise our movements."

Another one of the scientists, Macro, pondered the dilemma. "How about....Never mind."

"What?" Ribo asked.

"A stupid thought. Forget about it."

"Nothing's stupid unless it goes unsaid."

Marco shrugged. "Well, if we can't get in through the gates, how about where they dump the shit? I mean those damned citadels are big. A lot of food goes in there, and I know they've got to do something with all that waste."

Ribo, standing on the side at the front, hid a chuckle. She thought it would have been rude to laugh. "We've tried that. I just thanked the Gods I wasn't part of that *shitty* mission, so to speak." She turned to look at Macro.

Macro showed no emotions. Ribo stifled another laugh. "Anyway, I like the way you're thinking. We need creativity here. I've always said it'll be you guys in the lab that win this war; not us soldiers."

Ribo started to move, then reached to feel behind her. "Could've sworn somebody tied a weight to my ass." She moved quicker now, back to the normal hurried shuffle. "Anyway, Macro, get your ass busy. Think of crazy things like that. Stick your head in a cesspool, or lick some glue, or whatever the hell you need to do so that you think like those aliens do. Get your mind working like theirs, and maybe, just maybe, you'll crack that system. Do that, and their ass is mine! Get us in there undetected and I'll win this war."

"You can count on it, sir. If I have to eat their shit, I'll do it. Those codes will fall like the Roman Empire."

Ribo stopped dead, slowly turning back. "The goddamn Roman Empire took four or five centuries to fall, Macro. I don't have that kind of time. How about we stick to somebody like Custer? Have 'em fall like General Custer at Little Big Horn."

"Yes, sir!"

Ribo paused to receive a comm-link signal; it was headquarters. "Yes, sir. No, sir. I'm in a meeting with them now. Yes, sir. According to Cacid, they lost all of them? Yes, Teins's squad, too. All except Little Proton. And Cacid lost everyone. She was the only survivor. No, sir. I won't be long."

"Commander, we've got Proton here. You may wish to debrief him."

"He's there with you now, sir?"

"Right in front of me."

"Hold him, I'm coming over. I won't be fifteen minutes."

Nuc slid in next to Ribo. "What is it, Commander?"

"They've got Little Proton at headquarters. He reported on Teins and her unit. Like Cacid said, the whole unit was wiped out. Proton was the only survivor."

"Sorry to hear that, sir. I know you were close to Teins."

"Winning is all that matters. Teins knew that."

LITTLE PROTON RETURNS

January 6, 2054

Commander Ribo waited in her office, finding ways to stay awake, if not alert. Despite her efforts, sleep kept knocking on the door. *Teins, gone! And her whole unit with her. All except Proton.*

She had gone to headquarters, but Proton had already left. Ribs had instructed them to hold him, but he claimed he was too tired to stay awake. Headquarters related the information Proton had provided, but they wanted her to see if she could extract anything else. Proton was expected to report to her any minute.

The portal slid open and a guard announced her visitor. "Commander, we have Private Prot... sorry, sir. Private Ardle to see you. He's fresh from his rest, sir. The night watch brought him here straightaway."

Ribo forced a crack on what only a few of her men called a face. "Send Little Proton in, Sergeant."

"Yes, sir," he snapped.

Nerves danced all over Proton's body, making him a jumbled mess. Ribo laughed when she saw him. "At ease, soldier. I promise, I won't eat you."

Proton relaxed. "Sir, about the report, I..."

"I've already heard about the casualties. I spoke to Headquarters. Now, tell me in your own words what happened. Don't worry about formalities. Just think hard, take your time, and get it right. This is important. We're counting on you. And wherever she is, Teins is counting on you. She put everything into that mission. She put her life into it." Ribo thought that if the boy could have shed tears he would have.

He let his arms relax, took a deep breath, then looked Ribo in the eyes. "We got in all right, sir. It was a dark room, but we could see. Then we hit a barrier, so we made our way to the chute and went down to the fourth level."

Proton choked up. "Everybody was on the floor except me. I got caught up and was trying to get undone when the attack happened. I saw it all, sir. No doubt about it, it was an ambush. They were waiting for us, and they had stuff I've never seen."

Ribo questioned him for almost an hour, going over each part numerous times and asking questions in a variety of ways. Finally satisfied, she rested a moment in silence.

"Proton, I want you to go straight to Doctor Phage's lab. No stopping. No talking to anyone. He'll want to do some tests, possibly some scans, and he may want to question you some more. Don't worry, though, this is to try and uncover some clue as to how they knew we were coming. You're *not* in trouble. Understand?"

"Yes, sir," Proton said.

"One more thing, Proton. Stop and pick up whatever you wore as protective gear on the mission. Phage may want to see those things as well."

"Yes, sir," Proton said, and slipped through the portal.

As it turned out, Ribo joined Doctor Phage before Proton showed up. She wanted to hear what Phage thought. Besides, he had sent her a message earlier and said it was urgent.

"You were right, there is someone tipping them off," Phage said, as Ribo walked in.

Ribo sank. Of all things she anticipated hearing, this was the worst. "Who? Do you know who yet?"

"All of us," Phage said.

The commander furrowed her brow. "What the hell do you mean?" Ribo asked. "Explain."

"They have developed a sophisticated tag. It's far beyond anything we have. All they need to do is hit one of us. The tag then takes the readings of damned near everything you can think of and forms a profile. That profile is then fed into their computers. Once they have this information, if any one of us enters a citadel equipped with a similar defense system, we're picked up immediately by their tracers. And not just picked up, but targeted. They know *who* you are and *where* you are the whole time, so there's no sneaking around once you're in." Phage sighed. "It's foolproof, Commander. I can't break it."

Ribo fumed. "I don't know the word *can't*, Doctor Phage. It isn't in my dictionary. And I don't expect you to become too familiar with it either, at least not when you're around me. Military law does not prevent me from sending a lab director to the front lines."

Phage's shock was visible. "Yes, sir, Commander Ribo. I'll get you the answers."

As she was about to slide through the portal, Ribo turned. "Director?"

The doctor looked at her as if his fate were sealed.

"Suppose we go to new citadels? You said if we enter a citadel with the same defense system. Suppose they do not have the same system? What if they haven't fed our profile into a new citadel yet?"

The director scratched an imaginary chin. Some people would die to have no chin, others had a witch's profile, replete with warts. "A good thought, Commander. It would require a scouting report to test the theory. Should we risk another, after what happened with Captain Teins?"

"You let me worry about risk. Just keep up your end."

NEW PLAN

Ribo slipped into her command post and prepared to meet Oxy and De. She had called both of them using the comm link on the way over. *Should have planned for some rest time*, she thought, her body already sagging. Before she had a chance to think more about rest, Oxy entered.

Still the same old Oxy.

"You ever ask before entering, Ox?" Ribo tried to keep the frustration from her voice but she thought the tiredness might have shown.

"I ask my daughters."

Ribs felt the laughter rumbling in her body. "It's a good thing. From what I remember of the girls, they'd have your ass if you didn't knock. By the way, seen De?"

"She's coming. Saw her on my way over here. What's up? We going somewhere?"

A knock on the door was followed by, "May I come in, Commander?"

Ribo let her silent stare focus on Oxy for a long moment before she answered. "Come in, De. Sorry for the hesitation, I just wanted to let Ox observe the proper way to enter his commander's quarters. Seems like he forgets how to knock when it's anyone but his daughters."

De looked as if she were withholding a grin. "Knowing his daughters, sir. I can see why."

Ribo looked at both of them, rigid as rocks. "I need a dozen scouting teams. There'll be no attempt at breach on any of these missions. This is scouting *only*. Am I clear on this?"

"Yes, sir," came the reply from both of them.

"I'll leave the specifics to you, but I want to limit the search to citadels in our immediate vicinity. We need to be close to central if we're ever going to pull this off."

"What are we looking for, Commander?" De asked.

Commander Ribo stabbed De with her glare. "Did you think I wasn't going to tell you, soldier?"

"Sorry, sir. Won't happen again."

"We're looking for an entry point. An *unguarded* entry point to be specific. Security has gotten tight everywhere, so we want to steer clear of air filtration, ventilation, waste, and all the normal points. We need something new, and we need it in one of the citadels I've marked for you in the plans. You'll have them shortly."

"Time, sir?" Ox asked.

"As soon as possible, Ox. I intend to win this goddamned war. Not just come out on top of a skirmish here and there. I don't want someone far in the future to talk about Commander Ribo— whoever the hell she was—winning a minor skirmish at Colon Creek in 2054, or some shit like that. And yes, that pun was intended. Instead, I want them to say, Commander Ribo, the one who won the goddamned war. The one who drove those alien bastards right off this planet."

"Yes, sir," they both replied.

Ribo seemed lost for a while. "Sir," Ox said, "if there's nothing else, I'll get my teams ready. They'll be dispatched by morning."

"Same, sir," De said.

"Dismissed."

SCOUTS RETURN

June 14, 2054

I t had been a long time since Oxy and De set out on their missions. A soldier named Lei returned from a three-day reconnaissance. She seemed to be dragging.

"You look a little ragged, scout." Oxy loved to tease. Lei had been out for days, searching everywhere for a break in the enemy's defenses— she and half a dozen others. They had looked for weeks and found nothing. Nada. Niente.

"Won't be so cocky, after I deliver the report, Ox." If she could have smiled her grin would have spread from the legendary ear to ear. Suffering changed people though, took away more than life sometimes.

"You found something?"

"Found it," she said. "Found it all right. We've got us an unguarded entry spot."

An entry was important. At least, an unguarded entry was. They could always get in through the air ducts or waste disposal system, but security was tight there. Real tight. An unguarded entry was huge!

Three others joined in the applause and rousing cheers. "Hurry up then," Oxy said. "Get that report in. Ribs might even buy tonight when she hears this."

It had been a long time since any entry into the enemy camp had been found. They had sued for peace on a number of occasions, and though they thought to have been operating under a peaceful co-existence, the enemy always attacked. Always came back to kill. Whole clans had been wiped out. Whole races!

Long ago the enemy had developed shields that defied all resistance. They were like magical barriers, and even though all barriers had weaknesses and all shields had gaps, they hadn't been able to find a way to exploit what the enemy had developed.

Lei couldn't frown, but her lips would have turned down if they could have. "Don't get excited yet. It's an entry, but it's not ideal. They'll likely be waiting. Remember what happened the last time?"

The cheers stopped as each of them nodded. They remembered all right. They remembered losing half their own squad and two full divisions besides.

"We ever figure out how they knew we were coming? I mean, they had to know. Somebody had to tip them."

Oxy bulled his way through. "We're not starting that speculation again. I said it before. Nobody in this unit is dirty." He spun around, almost like a whirlwind, taking each one's measure. "If I hear it one more time, I swear by all that's holy, I'll put you in the death squad. There, it won't matter if somebody's dirty, 'cause you will all die anyway."

When he was satisfied he'd made the point, he turned back to Lei. "Before you get to Ribs, tell us about it. Where's the entry? How far to the headquarters?"

Again the sadness and gloom. "It's about as far away as you can get, Ox. You know where those two big pillars rise up out of that series of canyons?"

"I know," he said, losing some of his glee as he did.

"Well, once we got to the top, that was only the beginning. I went in and scouted. Figured I damned near got spotted a dozen times, too. Thought I saw some Abs, but couldn't be sure. Anyway, a small group could make it, maybe five or six. I wouldn't take any more than that."

She took time to look at the others while she spoke. "Two ways to go, fellas. Fightin' our way through every manner of God-awful terrain you can imagine or on the river."

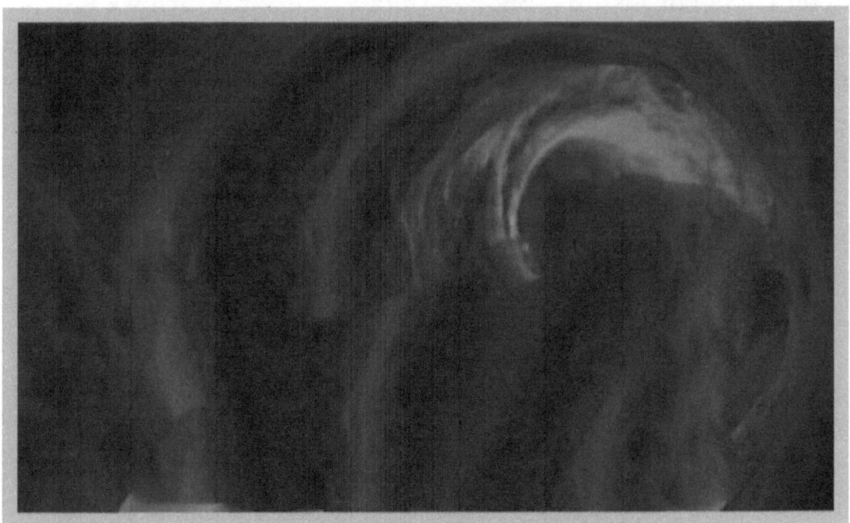
Dark tunnels

"Aw, shit!" someone yelled.

"Yeah, aw shit is right," Lei said. She saw it had been Rep, the "aw shit" guy, and she knew he'd been through it before. "It won't be pretty. It won't be easy. But it's the best way in, and the safest. At least we know what we face on the river. Less chance of getting spotted, too."

Oxy slumped. "Go see Ribs," he said. "She'll be waiting. Besides, she might have another idea. Tell her what your plan is and see what she says."

As Lei hustled off, he hollered to her. "Lei, ask her how much time we've got before we leave. Tell her I've got to get a crack team together. That'll take a while, week or two, at least."

"Good luck with that timing," she said, and hurried to see Ribs.

"Hey, Ox, what're Abs?" a new recruit asked.

Ox hated to laugh, though people said it felt good. "Abs are Abs, boy." He didn't even know this one's name yet. Fresh from the *factory*. "You'll learn as you get experience. Everything's an acronym around here. We've got Ab's, B's, Big E's, Thunder Quads, which we just call quads and a whole host of others." Ox knew the boy would be confused; he remembered his first month, fresh from training. "Have you ever heard soldiers holler out names or get heavy-winded in battle? No, I'd guess not. Acronyms! That's what we live by here, boy."

PREPARATIONS FOR ASSAULT

Commander Ribo signaled for the portal to slide open, not missing a beat as she hurried through, Ox and De on her tail. "Doctor Phage, I've brought two of my top leaders with me. They'll be spearheading the mission, so I want them to hear it firsthand."

Phage silently went to work preparing the demonstration. "I have shown this to Commander Ribo, and of course, to High Command. No one else, though."

The doctor fiddled with some items from his lab, then he signaled Ox and De to join him. "Look through the microscope. See that tag? We found that on Private Ardle. I believe you know him as Little Proton. It is a specialized tag that the enemy has used to mark us. Their tracers can pick this up the moment we enter any citadel. That's how they've been spotting us."

"I'll be damned," Ribo said. "Anything we can do about it?"

"We'll do a complete sweep of all your men prior to the mission to eliminate any tags they might have. Actually, we'll be modifying what you have so that it will transmit a different signal to the aliens."

Ox was busy thinking, but De perked up. "How's that possible, Doctor? I've been on some missions where we've had new blood fresh from the factory, and they still picked us up. Those new recruits couldn't have been tagged before."

Phage pointed his finger to an example of a typical entry he had laid out. "My theory is that they have something set up to mark us as we enter. Almost like a security system that tries to identify someone leaving an area, only in reverse. When any of us enter, we are somehow tagged. It shouldn't matter, though, as this technology will enable us to pass through undetected."

"So you're saying we can waltz around inside Citadel Central or Citadel Robbins, and those aliens won't notice?"

The doctor came alive with his animated gestures. "No! By all means, no. I'm saying the tracers won't pick you up, but if a squad of AB's or Quads comes roaring past and sees you, there better be a fire under your ass, my friend. You won't be invisible, just undetectable from tracers. To put it another way—I'm saying I can get you in undetected, but it will be up to you to stay that way."

Ribo pushed to the front. "Ox, De, unless you have more questions, let's get this going. I need a moment with the doctor, then I'll be out to see you."

~

"Ox, I've got to go take care of some shit before we go," De said. "Be back soon."

Six soldiers waited to greet Ox as he emerged. The youngest one spoke. "Good morning, sir. Been with Ribs?"

"I've been with Commander Ribo, if that's who you mean?"

"Yes, sir. No disrespect meant, sir. Just that... Ribs? Where did she ever get a name like that anyway?"

Ox laughed. "If you want to stay on the safe side of life, don't ever ask her. Ribo is her real name, though I don't know where that came from either. You know how parents are with names. Sometimes I think they just throw a bunch of names In a name-pool and pick one out when you come into this world. Otherwise how the hell did I end up with Oxy? Anyway, as far as Ribs goes, you address her as Commander Ribo, and if you ever get unfortunate enough to get on her good side, you'll have the privilege of calling her Ribs."

"I'll stick to Commander Ribo, I think. By the way, Ox, when are we going in?"

"You're testing my knowledge base today, Soldier. Have you seen Ribs talking to me? I suspect it'll be soon, though. Sooner rather than later, that's for sure. The enemy is kickin' our ass and we need to do something drastic. We need a win bad."

The soldier straightened and prepared to salute. "Shit! She's comin'."

Oxy spun like a top. Ribs moved across the field like she still wore the colors. Nothing cut her style. "Morning, Commander Ribo."

"Ox, are you ready?" The presence of command shined through.

"Not yet, sir, but we're working on it. Before I joined you this morning at the lab, I arranged a group. Figured you'd want us to leave soon. I got a half a patrol of top-notch guns ready to go at your command."

The commander saw De returning, and waited until she joined with her men. Ribs slowly assessed each soldier like a toy for sale. "You're taking a lot more than six, Ox. You too, Dee. I'm sending you in with a dozen patrols. Most of them will be used for decoys."

De began to protest but Ribo forestalled her. "Sad as that might be, De, it's my decision and it has to be done."

"Yes, sir," De said, and adopted a smile. Whether it was real or not, only she knew, but she put on a good show. De was like that, an obedient soldier.

Her name was De, but Ribo often called her Dee. Ribo said De's parents must have gotten tired of spelling and dropped the last 'e'.

Ox thought he remembered choking. "What! A dozen patrols is too many. They'll have tracers on our ass before we even get to the river. I don't care what Phage says about tags, I'm not buying that we'll be able to fool their tracers."

Ribs nodded. "I'm worried myself. That's why we're going to back up the dozen patrols with a full division. They will be the real decoys."

"A whole damned division? Who the hell did you clone to get them?" Oxy would have laughed, but the thought of another division going in almost frightened him. "I'm confused, Commander. You better help me out. I never was real good at the planning, but you know that. Why risk so much?"

Ribs never laughed— almost never. "I think we cloned you, Ox." A sort of snicker escaped before the commander found herself. "Ox, you'll have half a patrol, like you asked for. I'm also sending Dee in with her own crack team."

Ribs looked to the side. "You'll both will go in under cover. Full stealth. I mean *full*. You'll have ample time to get in and up through the canyons before we send in the decoys. The way I figure this— despite what the good doctor says—is they are going to detect you, whether it's with tracers, or something else. Some kind of alarm system."

She noted their suspicion. "Yes, alarm system. I refuse to believe we have any spies in our troops. I've given this plenty of thought. Nobody gave us away." The pause felt like a scolding. "Anyway, by the time you get above the canyons, I'd bet they know you've breached the system, so that's when I'm sending in the decoys. We are going to mount a full-scale attack at the breach and push them through."

"Shit, Ribs, that's gonna cost us. If they get the B's or the Thunder Quads down there, we might lose the whole division."

"Phage has convinced High Command that this is our best shot. They..." The commander paused, leaving her thoughts in the air.

"What is it, Commander?" De asked. "Is there something you're not telling us?"

Ribo motioned them aside. "High Command says we're going in strong. Real strong. They are so convinced that this is the big one, that they are committing forty five divisions. Hitting a whole sector of citadels at once."

"What! Are they goddamned nuts?" Ox paced in circles. "We can't afford to risk so much. Suppose they—"

"Suppose they what?" Ribs bit the words, but it felt to Ox and De like she was biting them instead. "The mission is paramount. The mission is all important. The mission is sacred." That pause again. The silent scolding. Ox winced. "High Command says we *must go* and that *we must succeed.* If we fail this time, it might be the end."

Ox wore a dejected look. "I'm going home to get some dinner. You going to the labs, Ribs?"

"I wouldn't if I didn't have to, Ox, but I've got to see Phage."

RESEARCH STRATEGY

"Commander Ribo," Nuc said. "They want you in Research ASAP."

"News, soldier?" she asked, but he had already turned in the direction of the lab. Nuc was one of Commander Ribo's oldest friends, but she still referred to him as *soldier* while on duty.

Nuc spun around at her question. "Sealed tight as a duck's ass, sir. I got nothing from them." He accompanied her to the lab. "You'll let me know if it's anything special, sir?"

The commander paused before entering. Nuc wouldn't be allowed inside. "If you see me doing double-duty, you'll know it's something important. But I suspect I'll be resting tonight."

"Yes, sir," Nuc said, and headed back to the barracks.

"Welcome, Commander Ribo. Doctor Phage has been waiting to address us."

Ribo had no patience. "Spit it out, Phage."

Phage held something up for all to see. "This device will allow us to neutralize their tags and their tracers. We were fortunate enough to have discovered a nearly invisible, undetectable tag on one of the soldiers that returned from the last patrol. From what we learned, we can now truly neutralize them. If we wanted to, we could send this same soldier back in and his tag wouldn't show up."

"Why didn't we know this before?" Ribs asked, her tone demanding an answer.

Phage nearly buckled. There was that searing question from Ribo.

"Just discovered it, sir. We—"

"Just discovered it where? I know of no patrol with a survivor of late. Your answer had better be truthful, Phage." Ribo's question forced him to face her.

"Sir, we took a closer look at Proton's tag. It seems, sir, that their technology was more advanced than we originally thought. The tag we originally found on Proton had another tag inside of it."

The information piqued Ribo's interest. "Go on, Doctor."

"I presume that they felt we would stop looking once we discovered the initial tag. And, in fact, we did stop. It was only by chance that I went back to this for further study. That's when I found this secondary, and more difficult-to-detect, tag. It is nearly invisible, sir."

"How does this help us, Doctor Phage?"

"Sir, they may be more advanced than us, but they haven't made anything yet that we can't duplicate. I have been able to recreate the tag for our own use."

Muttering from the room rose in a crescendo. "Better yet, we have discovered a way to disrupt their communications. They will not be able to signal for help or send for reinforcements.

"And you think that's what they did before? On the last strike? You think that they somehow signaled their headquarters—even though we detected no communications activity—and that headquarters then reinforced the citadels that we had not attacked yet?

"That's it exactly, sir. It's the only answer."

"Doctor, I'm not a scientist, but I have learned that there is always more than one answer. Always. If someone tries to tell you that the only answer to one plus one is two, you are looking at a moron."

"Excuse me, sir, but that is the only answer."

Ribo's look scolded him. "If you were to put one cat and one rat into a cage, Doctor, it's true that there would be two animals in there. But the next morning only one would emerge. Remember that when you look for answers. I don't want us to be the rats."

"No, sir. Neither do I."

"This better be good, Phage. I'm sending some of my top men in on this one."

"Yes, sir."

Ribs slid out the portal, already on the comm link to Ox.

TIME AT HOME

If it had been proper military procedure, Oxy would have stumbled through the door. He was that tired, but he knew the sight of his beloved twins—Norrie and Dolly—would fill him with energy, enough at least to play a few games with them. He felt the vibrations through the floor as they rushed to greet him.

"Hello, Daddy." That would be Dolly. He couldn't tell them apart physically, but he could by personality. Ox's wife, Linna, swore they looked different, but when pressed she couldn't identify one over the other.

"Daddy!" Ah, the more exuberant Norrie. Ox smiled when she wrapped her arms around him and squeezed. Linna insisted she should have been called "Little Ox," hardly a nickname for one of the sweet gender, but in principle he couldn't disagree. Although she looked exactly like Linna, she tried to mimic Ox with everything she did.

"How are my sweet babies tonight? Did you miss daddy?"

"We missed you," echoed from both at once.

It was times like this when he definitely couldn't tell one from the other. If he turned away and they switched positions he would have been lost. "Ah, my little clones, what did you do today? Mommy teach you anything?"

If they hadn't been so happy he thought they might have frowned. "We had to learn junk," Dolly said.

"Real junk," said Norrie. "Stuff we'll never use."

"What do you mean, never use? Who told you nonsense like that? Everything you learn is for a reason. It—"

"Uh uh. I heard mommy say that if your mission fails, we're all going to die."

Ox nearly died himself. "Linna! What the hell are you doing talking like that in front of them? They're goddamned babies!"

"Watch your words!" she shot back. "Besides, I wasn't talking in front of them. If they heard me, then they were snooping. You know I'd never say something like that while they were around."

Oxy spun toward them, picking up a tinge of anger as he did. "Were you? Have you been snooping again?"

Norrie fessed up. Coyly. Shyly. Her response was barely audible. "I guess you might call it that."

"Uh huh," came from Dolly.

"I swear, girls, if I catch you snooping again, you're gonna get it."

The message arrived so fast he thought it must have slid into his brain unnoticed. "Now, Ox. Need you at headquarters."

"Gotta go," he said.

"Are we all going to die?" he heard Norrie shout as he exited.

"No!"*Goddamnit, baby, I hope not*, he thought, and raced to see the commander.

BATTLE

Ox and De traded ideas then stood at the ready. The countdown had begun. "Ready, soldiers?" Ox shouted back to both groups. They were ready. He knew that. All they had to do was wait for the signal that the others were in place. He turned to De.

"A whole damned division! Guess Ribs is serious this time."

"Ribs is always serious. Christ's sake, look what we lost on the last attack."

Ox cleared his mind. Ribs sometimes got that imperious tone about her, and when that happened there was no talking to her. He wondered if it was her way of dealing with things. The pressure of the mission coming through. It showed up in everyone, just in different ways. He knew that his own frustrations came out with his babies. Little damned clones is what they were. Thinking about them brought sorrow.

I didn't even get a chance to say the proper farewells. Just in case. Aw shit, no sense thinking like that now. This mission would succeed. Had to!

De interrupted his ruminations. "Ribs is announcing that we're ready. All in place."

Oxy did a last check, then prepped himself. "All right. Prepare to launch. Check the chutes. We'll be floating out there, targets for anyone with a laser scope or even a big hair blower." They all laughed at that. Needed that, the laughter. "Go!" Ox yelled, then jumped himself.

The trip down had been uneventful, an auspicious beginning. When the last one landed, Oxy took command. "De, take the right flank. Strip off anything you don't need. I don't want one goddamned thing clanking or clinging or otherwise drawing attention to us. If tracers pick us up, I think you all know what that means. And I'll personally kill the first mother's son that trips an alarm." A steely gaze froze the front line of soldiers. "All right, then. Let's go. We're going in slow. Be steady. Be silent."

A small forest spread over uneven terrain lined the approach, but nothing difficult. De came back with the report. "It's there, Ox. Just like Lei said it was. It's a breach as big as a damned launch site. I can see where the river drains, too. We could use it as a marker. Follow it up."

Oxy thought about that, but dismissed it. "If they're expecting us, they'll have men stationed there. Damn, De, you know that. We'll have to go in then quickly move to the terrain. Get some cover. Once Ribs brings the decoys in and draws their attention, then we could risk the river. But even then, we'll have to check it out first."

"You're the boss," De said. "But let's go. I'm getting anxious."

The signal went out silently, and soon the two patrols crept in toward the gap in the shield. Ox halted the troop a short distance away, bringing the field into close-range vision.

"Everything all right?" De asked.

"Looks good," he said. "I would have felt better if this were a fresher breach, but with as few as we've found of late, guess we can't be choosy." He scanned for a while longer. "Can't see anything. If they've got soldiers there, they're doing a damned good job of camouflage. Better than ours could do."

"Let's do it, Ox. I'm tired of waiting," one of the men in his group said.

Oxy turned his stern look to De, then to all of them. "Listen up. That's just the kind of shit-eating attitude that will get us killed. I don't care what happens. We've got to be soldiers. Got to act like soldiers. Got to think like soldiers all the time. Got that?" He started to turn then mumbled. "Goddamned impatience will get us all killed."

Rough terrain and even some rusty-hued ridges capped the entrance, but Ox could see underneath, where the real breach was. *So they are already trying to cover it up,* he thought. So much for complete surprise, though that was always more of a pipe dream than reality in his head. "We got some guards," he said. "Not many, it's early yet. If we can take them out, sneak in, then get the decoys in here fast, it might fool 'em." *Might.*

Ox took the right flank, De the left. Ten more patrols waited for the signal to enter the breach. "We'll slip in and put the stranglehold on them, De. Got that? No noise."

De signaled from her side that she understood. From here on out, there would be no comm-links; no communication at all except whispers and body signals. De signed for Trace and his men to veer left. She would approach head on by herself. They wouldn't expect a lone enemy to present a problem.

She saw them staring at her, probably wondering what one soldier was doing trying to enter a citadel. When she felt certain she had their attention, she signaled for Trace to act. He and his men slipped in and finished them off before they could draw a weapon or call for help.

Ox raced to her side, fuming. "Goddamned dangerous ploy, De.

Showing yourself like you did. How the hell do we know they didn't call ahead, warn them?"

"We don't know yet, Ox, but if we wait a few minutes, we'll be able to tell. If they sent an alert, reinforcements will be here right away, and we can back out without losing any men. If no one comes, we can be pretty damned sure that they never made that call."

A tumultuous grumble festered inside of Ox. "I still don't like it, De. From here on out, you'll clear things with me before you try some crazy scheme."

"Yes, sir," De said.

Her response had a little too much snap in it for Ox's liking. She was just the type to ruin a mission like this, and he wondered again why Ribs had burdened him with her insubordinate ass.

A flash of light, almost like a bioluminescent spark, alerted the remaining ten patrols that they could now enter. It would be their job to follow Ox and De, and draw the fire of any aliens who happened to stumble onto the two primaries. Behind them would be an entire division, ready to storm the citadel, throwing their bodies against the breach at all costs. *Goddamn what a waste,* Ox thought.

The citadels were huge. It wasn't so different than moving through an entire city. Structures stacked up like mountains, forests sprinkled throughout, as if someone planted them by hand, and rivers, so many goddamned rivers—and all of them stinking like shit. Like alien shit.

They made it through the first phase with no problem, no sightings of the enemy. Now they faced the tower, a tough climb under any conditions. But having to worry about aliens took it from tough to torturous.

"Split up?" De asked, keeping the noise to a minimum.

Ox signaled a *yes,* then headed toward the right wall. He tapped De on the shoulder. "Follow the river if you can. That way we can meet at the top. And remember, De. No stopping. A wounded soldier is a dead soldier on this trip."

"I know. See you at the top."

Scaling the tower was like climbing a glass wall, a glass wall with sentinels that popped up every few minutes. Ox issued the signal to take cover once again, the third time in less than five minutes. They seemed to be hitting more sentinels the higher they climbed. The good thing, though, was no alarms had gone off. They hadn't bee spotted yet.

As soon as the way was clear, they began climbing again. Faster. He figured they were about halfway up when he heard the first alarm. The signal went out immediately to hide, and even that nearly proved too late. No sooner had they slipped into camouflage, then a full squadron of Thunder Quads came racing past.

"Christ's sake Thun—"

Enzo's words were cut off by Ox smothering him. *Another word and you're dead*, he signaled.

Ox knew they were all afraid. Hell, fear had crept up on him, too. He watched in horror as AB's, B's, and more and more Thunder Quads rolled by, all armed to the teeth, ready to kill. He wondered why they were bypassing him. He knew the decoys must have tripped an alarm somehow, but they should have been able to detect them once they were alerted.

Thoughts of the decoys flooded his mind. Fresh from the factory, all of them, where they churned out new troops like a bottling plant. Nothing but damned kids. Each one came equipped with the latest technological warfare, but with a mind so fresh and green and ideological that it pained him to see it. Pained him to see them grow so fast. So violently.

There were better ways, he knew. Better ways to live than this, but the goddamned aliens wouldn't let them live. Wouldn't let them exist, even. No, they wanted them all dead. All or nothing. It was war to the end. *If that's the way the bastards want it, that's the way it'll be. We'll fry those—*

A tap on his shoulder brought him upright. "What is it, Corporal?"

"Sir, the rear scout reports heavy engagement with the decoys. It... it sounds like a massacre, sir."

Ox risked the worst of breaches. He turned his comm-link on to listen only, headset mode. He heard the screams, the death cries. Heard the devastation. The patrol leaders were calling for help, asking for reinforcements. Ox knew there would be none coming. He only hoped that this was another decoy to trick the aliens. He hoped that Ribs had not told them to expect help.

"God bless them," Ox said, and turned off his comm-link. "All right, Enzo, let's move out. Brave soldiers gave us this time to get free, let's not waste it."

"Yes, sir," Enzo said, and hurried to get his gear.

Ox issued the signal to advance. A silent one. Silence marked the day now. De would be doing the same with her patrol. *Provided she survived,* Ox thought.

~

"De! They're coming. Quads!"

"Take cover," she said, then issued the signal for silence.

De heard them coming, like the rumbling in the sky before a storm. Shivers struck her when the AB's went soaring past. As battle-scarred veterans of many campaigns, they presented perhaps the most formidable challenge. All of them were dangerous, though, especially the Quads.

The shrieks of her companions in the decoys rang in her ears, a sound that would haunt her forever. When the flow of alien armies finally stopped, De signaled the move. They needed out of here and fast. She hugged the outer rim, hoping to avoid any contact. As they negotiated a particularly delicate turn, one of Trace's men hit the transmit button on his comm-link.

De spun around, fire inside of her. She could almost hear the Quads stop and listen. Regardless, she knew they'd be coming now. They might have missed them as silent stones, hiding in nooks and crannies, but they weren't so incompetent as to miss a comm-link signal.

"Run, Trace!.......

Trace scanned the terrain with a glance. Rivers were everywhere, and he'd never been a good swimmer, but there were also plenty of ways across those rivers, huge branch-like tentacles that he and his men could run on, providing they were balanced enough.

Trace started out with a dash, as if he were running a race. His men followed suit.

"Hurry up, Trace," one shouted when he slowed down while crossing a raging torrent.

Within minutes, they had made it to the other side safely, jumped off, then hid in the recesses of a few alcoves. Trace did everything he knew of to control his breathing. Now was not time for noise. As he waited for a chance to escape unnoticed, he wondered how De and Oxy were making out.

T race was just calming down when he heard the unmistakable sound of Oxy, shouting orders. He dared a peek out from the alcove and saw Oxy and De racing toward him with their patrols, and a full squadron of Thunder Quads on their asses.

"Run, Trace! Get the hell out of here!" De yelled.

Trace wasted no time. He signaled his men to scatter, then he rushed out of hiding and made a break for it.

D e and Ox ran for what seemed like days. *Maybe it was days,* De thought, not sure of anything anymore. Her maps gone, she had made an error and brought her troops around to where the battle was raging with those that had followed.

Thunder Quads and AB's swarmed the ten patrols, digging them out of hiding, from under flesh, out of the rivers, even among the bones. It didn't matter where they hid, the aliens always found them then overwhelmed them with sheer numbers, let alone firepower. She sighed. Her mistake might have cost them their lives.

She saw only one chance—get them to the darkest section of the tunnel, where the enemy couldn't spot them. With that in mind, she signaled them to follow her. It was a good suggestion, as no one could see more than a few feet in front of them. *If we can't see, then they can't.*

tunnel

Meanwhile, far below, bodies piled up at the breach, where Ribs had an entire division storming the gap. The corpses stacked one upon the other, until bloody flesh crowded the citadel, crammed against flesh and bone and other foreign matter.

Most of De's unit were dead now, dead or wounded, and on this mission that was one and the same. De screamed as she tore through a mass of flesh—some alive, most not. A river polluted with the worst of the species' waste lay a short distance ahead, and De made a break for it, dragging Trace along with her. "Come on, soldier. Get your ass out of here. We've got to hit the darkness."

They fought through four assaults, fortunate to have been seen by only the fresh alien troops, no AB's or Quads. For a time they seemed to be safe, although traipsing along the river proved to be a regretful decision. She had been following the stench for what seemed like miles and there wasn't any end in sight. De stopped short, flicking a signal to Trace.

Trace went still, then De sniffed the air. She didn't think sniffing would work, but she had to try since she couldn't see in this darkness, and she felt certain that the enemy would not make the mistake of breaking silence.

She sensed the attackers before she saw them or even heard them, and the Gods only knew she was not going to be able to smell them with that river of shit nearby. "We've got company, Trace. Run!" She tore off as she shouted the message.

Trace sped alongside her, but his energy seemed to deplete faster than hers.

Females had proved to be the strongest after all, De thought. But she had no time to relish the victory. They had stopped to rest in another dark alcove.

One of the soldiers, scared half to death, asked her. "De, what the hell was that?"

Her voice remained calm, measured as she answered the question, and at the same time addressed the soldiers who lived.

"Thunder Quads. I hit a band of T's earlier today and they weren't happy about it. Probably been tracking me ever since. At least I'm guessing so."

"Thanks for the warning," Trace said, his words coming out in labored pants. "I could have been out of here if I'd known you were on a suicide run."

De laughed. "Are there any other kind of runs?"

"Me, too," Chill said. "And to think, I volunteered for this, but I didn't plan on dying."

De thought of Trace and Chill, and of what Ribo had told them all about the risks. "The commander told everyone what to expect," she said.

"Yeah, yeah," Chill said, "He looked both directions, then went out on a run, reckless as always. Before he got fifty feet, he bought it.

De tapped Trace on the side and whispered. "See what reckless behavior brings? Do what I say and don't try anything stupid."

Trace nodded. "You got it," he said.

"I mean it," De said. "We've got time, so be careful. It's like Nuc says, 'We've got all the time in the world.' I'm not sure I believe that, but I *do* think we have *some* time."

A shot ripped past them tearing a hole in the flesh of a nearby corpse. Trace shivered.

De felt him quivering, and she whispered, "I don't think they saw us, but if these Thunder Quads have their way, we won't have *any* time."

～

"So what do we do?" Trace asked. "Do we stay here? Or do we make a break for it?"

"I say we make a break," De said, then she bolted from her hiding place and increased her pace, ducking a volley of fire. "Their aim is improving, Trace. Better pick up the speed."

Trace risked a glance behind him and almost dropped with fright. Seven Thunder Quads rounded the bend, unremitting in their hot pursuit.

Once agitated, the Quads proved to be relentless predators, and Trace didn't know if he had enough left in him to elude them today. He could barely catch his breath. "Go on ahead, De. I'll try to stay and hold them off." He could already feel his pace slowing.

De reached to grab him, though he tried to shake her off. "Hold on, Trace. There's a tunnel ahead. If we can stay alive for a few more minutes, we'll be safe. I've got a launcher waiting."

The thought of a launcher sent shock waves through him. *Was it true? Did she really have one this close?*

He had to trust her, had to push a little harder. He mustered every resource he could and massed it together for a final thrust, shaking off De's grip as he did. The strain was overwhelming, but soon he was alongside her again and holding his own. "How much farther? And no bullshit about it."

"Around that bend where the island splits the old chasm, then up a hill and into a cave. After that, we're home free."

He pushed harder, almost feeling the heat of the lasers whisking past him. Fear kept him from turning around. There was no way he wanted to see how close the Quads were.

De's encouragement had given him new hope; perhaps they could make it. After all, the bend wasn't far. He could maintain this pace long enough to get there.

The steep hill sounded ominous, though if De hadn't covered up anything by omission, it was a deed that could be done. Then the cave. He knew Quads hated caves, so they were pretty much safe if they just made it there, unless there were Battle Cells.

A shot nicked De's arm, ripping a piece of her as it went through the meaty part. "Goddamn!" she screamed, and crashed into a wall.

Trace ran to help, but she had straightened herself and resumed running almost immediately. "Go! Don't wait for me."

Trace hesitated, but De was in command. He had to follow orders. The commander would hurt him worse than the Quads if he disobeyed orders under fire, and Trace held no doubts about whether De would report him. She might be friendly and crazy while on a mission, but she'd report the slightest breach in orders. He saw the path splitting up ahead, and was just about to ask which one when he heard her shout.

"Take a right. Go."

The incline didn't seem too steep, but for this tired vessel it might prove to be the hurdle that killed him. The exertion level increased as he climbed and his pace slowed more than the path narrowed. The Thunder Quads' shots now had the added benefit of ricocheting off the walls. It was dark, too. How many might be hidden along the way. *I hope she knows what she's doing,* Trace thought, and dared a quick look to ensure De was still with him.

She had almost caught up, though the mass of Quads seemed to fill the tunnel behind her. "Don't stop for anything," she shouted, and Trace thought he saw her coax more speed from her tired body.

Trace wondered if they were running straight uphill now, but the prospect of Quads breathing down his back put fuel in his furnace. "How far, De?" he shouted without turning around.

~

"Just over the hill. Be ready." De fought to get more energy. As they neared the crest, she pulled an irritant from her pouch and put it in place. "Get on site, now!" she screamed, and pushed herself harder to catch up to Trace.

The Quads roared over the hill, death singing from every alien pore. De chanced a glance behind her and saw death only seconds away, then she pushed with all she had to reach the launch site. Life waited there. She rested in fate's hands now.

Just as the Quads reached for her, the launcher exploded, shooting her and Trace out at a velocity strong enough to rip flesh from bones.

"Hang on!" Trace shouted, and grabbed hold of De at the last second.

When the launcher went, it sent debris, refuse, and other things along with them. De collided with a gooey mass of something, cursing as it struck. She prayed it wasn't flesh. Through all of the tumbling and battering, she somehow managed to keep hold of Trace, who was just now coming to her senses, after passing out at launch.

Trace awoke seconds later. "Where are we?"

De analyzed the situation and realized they were almost out of control. She had been through a launch before. "Trace! Steer right. Watch for nets. They know we've launched, so defenses will be set."

Trace squeezed her, then shouted. "Don't worry, I've got it."

"It's no game, Trace. If we're caught we're dead." De kept a watchful eye on their path. "Here they come!" she warned. "Veer right!"

They both leaned as they steered clear of the nets, avoiding capture by a hair's breadth. A sigh of relief brought new life to De. "Good job, Trace. I didn't count on getting out of there alive."

"We wouldn't have if not for you," Trace said.

"Yeah, yeah. Enough of this sentimental bullshit. Let's get back to headquarters. Ribs will want a full report."

FINAL STRATEGY

Commander Ribo pored over the reports from all the patrols—all surviving patrols, a far fewer number than they began with. Ox and De made it back and a handful of others. Thirty-six patrols lost as well as dozens of divisions! Some of her best units were with them. Ribs gathered what she needed then headed toward the lab.

I'm gonna have Phage's ass.

The portal to the lab slid open to allow Ribo entry. "Phage! What the hell went wrong? Do you know how many men we lost?"

Phage seemed to be wearing a smile. It infuriated Ribo. "What the hell is there to smile about, mister?" She ignored the honorific.

"Sorry, Commander. I meant no disrespect. I questioned all the survivors and found nothing. Nothing that is until a few hours ago."

Phage signaled for a young scientist to move forward. "This is one of my new assistants. His natural curiosity drove him to study statistical data that I had not thought to look at, and I believe he has found the answer to what went wrong."

The doctor had Ribo's full attention. "Go on, but let the boy explain."

The young scientist flushed. "Well, sir. I pulled up all data on the citadels that we launched assaults on. I'm sure you know the extent of it, sir, but it numbered in the hundreds just in this sector. More elsewhere. Many more."

Ribo cringed, thinking of all the lost lives. All of the grieving survivors.

"I massaged that data from every angle, sir, and finally a pattern showed. The survivors—every one of them—came from citadels that we had never infiltrated before. In every case where we had previously entered a citadel, the entire assault team was lost. In every case that is, except Citadel Central, where Ox and De went."

The commander scowled at Phage. "I don't have time for my own analysis, Doctor What conclusions have you come to?"

"Since they picked up on every citadel where we had been before, that tells me that they are still marking us somehow. As to why Ox and De weren't picked up, I can't say. To venture a guess, they were the only ones subjected to sterilization, so something in the process got rid of whatever tag was on them."

Ribo took some time to digest the information. "Are you telling me, Doctor, that there was more than one tag on our men? Even more than the one tag that concealed another? And that you didn't find them?"

Phage nearly buckled under her scathing glare. "Yes, Commander. Actually, sir, if you recall, we found that second tag on Ardle; however, the device I designed to jam the signals should have stopped their tracers from picking them up."

"Find them! I want you to examine our troops until you can locate these tags and find a way to eliminate them."

ANOTHER NEW PLAN

Ribo stalked through the darkness of command headquarters. High Command wanted another strike, and nothing Ribs could do would change their minds. She roamed until the first crack of light shone through, like the sparkle in a baby's eye, then made her way to the lab. She was not going to lose more men, not like the previous assault. Losing a patrol was one thing, dozens of divisions something else.

Everyone stood to attention when the portal slid open at precisely 05:45. They all knew it would be Ribs. A beehive had less activity than the lab this morning, scientists and soldiers milling about, mingling, chatting about battlefield experience and practicalities with scientific theories and prototypes.

Ribo let the silence linger while she stared at them. This motley bunch represented their race's last hope. "Ideas?"

Ox was closer than anyone to Ribs, so perhaps it was appropriate that he spoke first. "Phage thinks he knows how it's done, Commander."

Ribs focused her predatory gaze on the doctor. "If you have something new, explain. If it's the same tired shit, forget it."

"It's new, Commander."

"Then explain."

"They are using our dead, Commander. I have finally determined that. They gather the dead, analyze them, take biological imprints then create a profile of our race. With the level of technology they have at their disposal they can not only tell what race we are, but they can get us down to a clan level. As long as they have this in place, none of us can enter without being detected."

"What about the sterilization you used on Ox and De? That apparently worked for them."

Phage denied it with every body movement. "No, sir. It actually didn't. To test it we sent two men from Ox's patrol back in, and they went to new citadels, not ones we had been to before. They didn't get far before the enemy came. AB's and Quads both. The determining factor was that the AB's didn't know exactly where they were, and they weren't waiting for them, but they were out on a search, so the alarm was tripped. Thank God one of the men escaped to give us the report."

Phage paced, while the rest of the room remained silent. Ribs let it stay that way. She always said silence was the best interrogator. "Sterilization takes away the specific tag for the tracer to pick up, so they can't pinpoint our location, but they know we're in there as soon as we breach the defenses."

Ribo acknowledged the information and paced while digesting this new data. "Thoughts, people. That's what a think-tank is for. Let's hear some thoughts." She thought she noticed one of the scientists about to say something, then stop. "You, she pointed him out. You have something to say?"

A thin rakish-looking scientist stood at attention, rigid with fear.

"Speak, boy. I don't bite."

"We need some way to disguise ourselves, sir. Put on a skin just like theirs. Maybe some sort of gelatinous mass that makes us look, smell, even taste like one of those stinking shits."

A round of cheers greeted his statement. Ox and De signaled agreement. Everyone did, the researchers, the think-tank guys, all of them.

"We're working on it already," Macro said.

Macro got his name from the automatic processes he developed during a major confrontation with the aliens.

It wouldn't do to show pride, but Ribs nearly did. "Whatever you come up with is going to have to resist probes and sensors as well. We don't know what they have, so we're going to have to make it as invisible as can be. I want our troops to look just like them when we go in. I want them to look so much like them that we could lie down and procreate with the ugly bastards. God forbid!" Ribs drew silent chuckles with that one.

"Ugly bastards is right," Ox said. "I'd kill myself first."

Doctor Phage chimed in with a thought. "I think this has given me an idea, Commander. Brilliant!"

"What, Phage?" Ribo asked, but the doctor. was already making his way toward the lab, three scientists dogging his tracks.

Ox watched them leave, then turned to Ribo. "Commander, I'll stay and work with them. Get some rest and we'll report any new developments."

Ribs stretched, reaching for some comfort to replace sleep. "I think I'm going to take you up on that, Ox. Call me, though. Don't hesitate."

"Yes, sir, Commander."

PHAGE COMES THROUGH

S ir, I heard a lot of whooping and shit-calling from research," her assistant said. "Maybe they have something."

"Stay alert. I'll go see." Ribs moved as quickly as her *mutant* body would allow. She knew what they called her. How they spoke about her when they thought she wasn't around. Hell, who hadn't done the same as a soldier. If you couldn't hate your commander, who could you hate?

The entry to the lab slid open like a waterfall being parted. She heard the celebrations going on—only a short distance to go now. *Did they have something?* Ribs let a jolt of excitement course her body and that naturally quickened her pace.

She thought of a scowl when she slipped through two more security zones with no guards. *They better by God have something, or I'll have some ass.* Phage, covered in lab slime, chatted with obvious admirers at the far side of the room.

Ribs veered in that direction, a determined set to her movement. "Director, what the hell is going on?" The conversations and merrymaking turned to silence and spread outward from the commander like ripples In a pond.

A shiver started at the head and ran down Director Phage's long thin frame. If he had been green he might have resembled a blade of grass. His entire career had been spent in the lab, dedicated to one purpose only: find the weapon that will win this war. It had been issued as a challenge since he entered the academy and it hung on plaques throughout the lab and around the campus as a reminder. His head felt like the rose on top of a long stem.

"Commander Ribo, we have it. This is it. This is the one we've been waiting for."

She denied herself the luxury of a premature smile. No jubilation until she had proof. Others, more experienced others, had led her astray before with tales of "the weapon," "the cure" and countless monikers they attached to false claims. "Clear the lab first. Then we can discuss what you *think* you have."

"All this time we've been focused on hiding ourselves. trying to find ways to avoid their defense systems, elude their tracers, outfight the AB's and Quads, and B's. Suppose we've been doing it wrong? Suppose for a minute, that we have been going about this backwards?"

"What the hell do you mean, Phage? How the hell else do we win a battle if we're getting picked off from the moment we enter the citadel? We have been successful in the past by inventing ways to avoid detection for a while, but never for long."

Phage quivered, and looked as if he was about to interrupt on numerous occasions but he didn't.

"All right, Phage. Let's hear what you've got to say. But it damned well better be good."

"I can guarantee us a quick access without detection, though we might have to wait six months or so, maybe even a year. Hide out until then."

Ribs signaled agreement, even if she didn't know it. There was that slight way her body twisted, the almost imperceptible nod of her head.

"Anyway, this time when we go in, it's not with the intention of battling it out one on one, or trying to win with superior numbers, and it's certainly not with attempting to overcome their technology—"

"Then what the hell is it, Phage? I'm tired of playing these games. I haven't slept in days, and I don't have time for bullshit."

"We go in and trigger the alarms ourselves."

Ribo almost exploded, so Phage forestalled her with a signal. "Wait, Commander, please. Before we trigger the alarms, we use something I've invented to give us the edge. The final edge. It is a membrane substance. Once we are close enough to a target, we can cover that target with it and it will trigger the alarm, but it will make their defense system think that they are us." Phage waited until this first part sunk in.

"Their tracers and their headquarters will pick up these false tags, and they'll send out the troops, the full complement: AB's, B's, Quads, all of them. But the difference is that this time their *own* troops will hunt them."

Ribs didn't look convinced. "They've got communications. Why won't their men signal that they're hitting the wrong targets?"

Phage felt exuberant. This was the brilliance of it all. "We will be turning their technology against them. They have hunted for so long by trusting their tracers and their other technological wonders, that if faced with a communique stating that a target is wrong, but their own systems telling them otherwise—they'll go with the system. You forget. How can a common soldier tell the chief what to do? It's even worse when dealing with a technological wonder like their defense system."

The commander remained unconvinced, then Phage said, "Sir, they have trusted their defense for so long, it is now the authority—it *is* their decision maker. They cannot override it."

"We'll need to try it out first," Ribs said.

"With this "tag," sir, we can do what we always wanted and more. Not only can we disguise ourselves to get entry, but we can then "tag" the enemy without their knowing. It can be programmed, then activated to make their Quads think their own troops are us."

Possibilities ran through Commander Ribo's mind. She thought about the countless ways the aliens could counter them, might prepare for them as they always had in the past. But if it did work? If it really could work....? She wouldn't let herself get that far ahead.

"Downside?" she asked.

"We have to be close to make it work. Probably too close."

"How do we know it will work, Director? I don't want my soldiers going in there thinking they're invisible only to show up on the enemy's board like goddamn Christmas lights."

Ribs thought the director looked sullen. "It will work, Commander. I can guarantee that."

"How can—"

"I already tried it out, sir. One of my men went in. It worked all right."

"Why so sad, Director? If you have the proof, I would think you would be ecstatic."

He nodded. "Like I said earlier, Commander, when you asked about the downside. We have to be close to activate it. We need one of us to activate each tag. Several would be better. The connection is a strange one, and it won't work unless we're near. That means that we are going to lose our own when we activate them."

Phage looked as if he might crumble. "Happy as I was at our success, Commander. It did not come without its price. That was my son who went in to try it out. He insisted."

Ribs understood. *More dead. But if it worked....* "We'll need volunteers."

"Yes, sir," he said, and gathered his things to leave.

ENEMY CAMP

"We're under attack in the west."

"How bad is it?" Forello paced the room while he talked. A habit he had picked up from his father, a lifer in the military.

"It's a damned siege. The entire coast is affected and the best we can do right now is try to contain them."

Forello bit his lower lip, paced more. "Any reason to believe they'll hit us here?"

Collins held back the frustration. And fear. "I already told you about Robbins and Joshua, and—"

"Isolated incidents. If I didn't know better, I'd swear they were decoys."

"But, sir, there are a few other cases. Just—"

"Listen to yourself! 'A few other cases' That is *exactly* what I'm talking about. A handful of losses doesn't amount to anything. God's sake, man! Look to the west. We've got bodies piled up in the streets."

Collins lowered his head. "What are your suggestions?"

"We still don't know what they used the last time, so I want everyone to undergo massive inoculations. Start in the west, but keep it going until we're done. No sense in entering this unprepared."

Forello kicked at a chair, knocked it sideways. "In the meantime, we're going all out against them. I want to bring out every weapon we have. I want all of our people armed. We're going to kick the shit out of these bastards."

"I'll get started right away," Collins said, and headed toward the door.

Forello grabbed his arm as he passed. "Collins, I don't want any of them alive. Do you understand me? Make sure you kill them all."

FINAL STRATEGY

March 15, 2055

Commander Ribo took her time strolling the dark corridors of headquarters, home for so long. Her meeting was to have started five minutes ago, but today she would be late. There was a first time for everything—and a last. The darkness had never caught her attention before, not like it did today. As she studied it she realized there was something beautiful about darkness. Something ominous, yet wonderfully relaxing.

She heard the soldier racing up behind her, so cut her ruminations short. "Yes, soldier. I know I'm late. Report back that I'm on my way."

"Yes, Commander."

The echoes of his leaving were soothing to her. It seemed as if nothing could disturb this morning. She took a full ten minutes to reach the meeting room, a cavernous hall that resembled an airplane hangar. Her soldiers stood at attention, stiff as stone columns. "Good morning, Ox, Nuc, De. Good to see you."

Ox must have suspected something, otherwise he would have

commented. Ribo let her gaze flow over each soldier, young and old alike. The children she never had. "Comm links on."

When she saw that everyone had hooked up, she continued. "I'm sure you know why you're here. This is a momentous occasion for our race. In the future they will look back upon today as the day that everything changed. The day we took back what the aliens had stolen from us." She let the emotions build, catching as many gazes as possible.

"You see here the leaders of a thousand divisions. Formidable, you might think. But we have launched massive assaults before. Imagine that each of you represents a division, then imagine that scene being played out in a thousand rooms around the globe." She saw the calculations and the wonderment that grew with the conclusions. "Yes, this is it. The final strike. Every able-bodied soul is going in today. We'll strike at citadels across the world.

"Many of you have children," she said, and saw their acknowledgment. "Today we will ensure that your children will have children and theirs after them. Today we will drive these aliens from our cities, and our towns, and our lands! Today will mark the day in history when countless generations of persecution came to an end. Because today, soldiers, we will win this damn war!"

A deafening roar filled the room, echoing off the walls only to resound again with each new shout. Ribo waited for it to settle down somewhat before she spoke again. "Those of you who have family, go home. Those of you with friends, say good-bye. Do what you have to do and meet back here at 13:00."

Nuc grabbed hold of Ribo before she could leave. "Don't think of leaving me out of this, Ribs."

"Commander Ribo, to you soldier."

"At this stage of the game it's Ribs. If this is the last one, I'm in."

Ribo let her silence scold him as she had done so many before. "You know you won't be back, Nuc."

"I know, Ribs. It's time. This is the one that counts. If I'm going out, I want to go out on the big one. Someday my kids or grandkids will read about me. Ol' Nuc, he led the big one, they'll say."

Ribo saw De coming up from the side. She didn't have time for all of this sentimental shit. "All right, Nuc. You've got it. I'll see you in the next world."

"Me too," he said, and hurried away just as De joined Ribs.

Ox watched the men scurrying from the room, but he was waiting for Ribs to finish with De. Soon Commander Ribo turned.

"I'm glad you didn't leave, Ox. I wanted to speak with you."

"You can't keep me out of this, Ribs."

"Ox, that's exactly what I'm doing." Ribs stopped his protest before he could voice it. "You are staying home with your family. Those twins are more important than one more soldier in the field."

"Not to my men, sir. I've got to be there to lead them."

"That's why I'm going," Ribo said. "I'm taking your place." Again, she had to stifle him. This time with a glare. "This is not debatable, soldier. This is not up for discussion. This is an order. And I swear, I'll have your ass arrested if you try to buck me."

Ox steamed in silence. "Why, Commander?"

"Because this is it, Ox. I've waited all my life for this day. I need you to stay home and chronicle it. Make sure I get honorable mention in the history books."

Ox choked back a few imaginary tears. "Okay. You got it." They stared at each other for a while, then Ox spoke again. "Permission to hug the commander, sir?"

"Permission granted," Ribs said, and squeezed him for all she was worth. *Why hadn't he done this before?*

"Get home, soldier. Take care of those girls."

"Good luck, Ribs." He started to leave then turned. "Sir, I always—"

"Home, Soldier. Go home."

"Yes, sir."

～

O*9:00 High Command Headquarters.*

"Commander Ribo, are your men ready?"

"Ready, sir."

"Issue the orders."

Ribs smiled. This was it. "Today, we attack!" she said, and led them toward their targets.

CITADEL JOSHUA (ENEMY CAMP)

August 1, 2055

Citadel Joshua burned from within. Fires raging. It couldn't stand long at these temperatures. None of them could, and it had already spread. Citadels Madison and Spinello had recently fallen, and the latest reports showed Orson and Milan failing quickly. Less obvious, but under heavy siege were citadels in Roma, Tokyo, NYC, London, Cairo, and Sao Paulo. Rescue teams worldwide remained on twenty-four hour alert. Suits and masks were now in short supply, but even with their gear, little hope remained.

A phone rang, and the doctor rushed to get it. The private line. An image flashed on his screen, then his heart sank. "What news?" he asked, not a hint of optimism in his voice.

"Nothing good, John. I just heard from Atlanta. It's out of control."

"How bad?"

"The worst. I'm leaving, John. Going home to spend time with Joan."

"But—" A flash of blue swallowed the screen, then nothing.

Doctor Robbins trod the corridor with shoulders slumped, feet shuffling. He pushed open the door to patient room #414, shook his head as he made his way slowly to the bed. He motioned everyone away and placed his hand on the boy's head.

Fever's wild. No change.

He had prescribed all the medication, followed by alcohol baths. Tried everything he knew, even old folk remedies, but nothing worked. "Joshua. Joshua, can you hear me?" Robbins knelt beside him now, but saw no recognition in his eyes.

The doctor turned, startled when the door burst open. Mrs. Nash charged across the room, flinging herself at the bed, arms clutching, grasping. Voice pleading between sobs and wails.

"Not my baby! Not him, too!"

Robbins tugged gently at her arm, though she had clamped onto the sheets like a vise. "Mrs. Nash, let's step outside. Give Joshua his rest." He patted her back as he spoke, ashamed at the little consolation he could offer.

"Doctor Robbins?" Joshua asked.

Robbins rushed to the other side of the bed, knelt and held the boy's hand. "Yes, Joshua. What is it?"

"Am I going to die?"

Guilt flushed Robbins' cheeks, coursed his veins. "I don't know, Joshua. I just—"

"Don't you dare say that!" Mrs. Nash nearly came across the bed at him, her nails looking now like the talons on an eagle.

"Timmy died. Mary too. Didn't she, Mom? I'm going to die, too. I can feel it."

Mrs. Nash wept in great heaving sobs. She yanked at her hair and a clump of it pulled free, leaving blood on her scalp. "I'm not going to let you die."

Doctor Robbins moved slowly now. He had been infected himself a few weeks ago. He patted Joshua's hand, then rubbed his damp head. "I'm afraid there is nothing that can be done, Joshua. You see, it is not them that is killing us. We are killing ourselves."

"What do you mean? That's a stupid thing to say!" Joshua's mother clawed at the doctor. "How can you let that happen? Why doesn't someone stop them?"

Joshua fell back asleep. Doctor Robbins reached to calm Mrs. Nash, then led her from the room. All of his muscles hurt, even his bones ached.

"You see, Mrs. Nash, it was the viruses. They finally figured out how to eliminate us, and they did it with such simplicity. They developed a means of tricking our body into thinking that our own cells were invaders. In that way, our own immune system, which has always been our primary means of defense, attacked our bodies. And we were left defenseless."

"What will I do without my baby? I've already lost Mary. How will I go on?"

Doctor Robbins shook his head slowly. "Mrs. Nash, I'm afraid you misunderstand. You won't have to worry for long. None of us will. It's not just Joshua who will die; it's all of us. We're all going to die, Mrs. Nash. They've won. The viruses have won."

I'm sure that some of you picked up on this. If you did, kudos; if not, I hope it made the reading experience better. In any case, I hope it did not *interfere* with the reading experience.

There is a growing debate as to whether viruses are alive. If they are, perhaps a scenario such as this is not too far fetched; if they're not, then this is an old man's imagination running wild.

Cast of Characters

De + Oxy + Ribo + Nuc + Lei + C + Acid (DNA) (deoxyribonucleic acid)

Macro + Phage (macrophage)

Pro + Teins = Proteins

Proton

Neurrie + Ron = Neuron

AB's = antibodies

B's = B-Cells

Thunder Quads = T-4's (killer t cells)

ACKNOWLEDGMENTS

It is with great honor that I give eternal gratitude to my wife and all four of my grandkids. They give me the inspiration to keep going.

ABOUT THE AUTHOR

Giacomo Giammatteo is the author of gritty crime dramas about murder, mystery, and family. He also writes non-fiction books including the No Mistakes Careers series, No Mistakes Publishing, No Mistakes Grammar, and No Mistakes Writing.

When Giacomo isn't writing, he's helping his wife take care of the animals on their sanctuary. At last count they had forty-five animals—eleven dogs, a horse, six cats, and twenty-six pigs.

Oh, and one crazy—and very large—wild boar, who takes walks with Giacomo every day and happens to also be his best buddy.

nomistakespublishing.com
gg@giacomog.com

ALSO BY GIACOMO GIAMMATTEO

You can see all of my books here.

And you can buy them on the platform of your choice here.

Nonfiction :

No Mistakes Resumes, Book I of No Mistakes Careers

No Mistakes Interviews, Book II of No Mistakes Careers

Misused Words, No Mistakes Grammar, Volume I

Misused Words for Business, No Mistakes Grammar, Volume II

More Misused Words, No Mistakes Grammar, Volume III

No Mistakes Writing, Volume I—Writing Shortcuts

How to Publish an eBook, No Mistakes Publishing, Volume I

How to Format an eBook, No Mistakes Publishing, Volume II

eBook Distribution, No Mistakes Publishing, Volume III

Uneducated

Fiction:

Friendship & Honor Series:

Murder Takes Time

Murder Has Consequences

Murder Takes Patience

Murder Is Invisible

Blood Flows South Series:

A Bullet For Carlos: A Connie Gianelli Mystery

Finding Family, a Novella

A Bullet From Dominic

Redemption Series:

Necessary Decisions: A Gino Cataldi Mystery

Old Wounds

Promises Kept, the Story of Number Two

Premeditated

OTHER BOOKS COMING SOON:

You can always see the current and coming-soon books on my website.

Fiction:

***A Promise of Vengeance* (Fantasy)**

My first fantasy, and the first book in a four-book series—the Rules of Vengeance. (Three are already written and the fourth is being outlined.)

A Hard Life, the Story of Tip Denton

***Memories for Sale* (mystery/sf)**

***The Joshua Citadel* (SF novella)**

Nonfiction:

Whiskers and Bear—Volume I of the Life on the Farm Series (sent to editor)

No Mistakes Writing, How to Write a Bestseller

Children's Books:

No Mistakes Grammar for Kids, Volume I—Much and Many (sent to editor)

No Mistakes Grammar for Kids, Volume II—Lie and Lay (sent to editor)

No Mistakes Grammar for Kids, Volume III—Then and Than (sent to editor)

Shinobi Goes to School—Life on the Farm for kids. (working on illustrations)

Get on the mailing list and you'll be sure to be notified of release dates and sales.

Mailing list

And don't forget to leave a review!

By the way, if you're an author and you liked the formatting in this book, you might consider us for your next book. Information can be obtained here.

www.ingramcontent.com/pod-product-compliance
Lightning Source LLC
Chambersburg PA
CBHW032050180726
48284CB00004B/1265